D0842576

Purchased from
Multnomah County Library
Title Wave Used Bookstore
216 NE Knott St, Portland, OR
503-988-5021

To Princess
Iris Harper Haynes
—*K. L.*

To my sisters
—*S. H.*

Text copyright © 2010 by Kate Lum
Illustrations copyright © 2010 by Sue Hellard

All rights reserved. No part of this book may be used or reproduced
in any manner whatsoever without written permission from the publisher,
except in the case of brief quotations embodied in critical articles or reviews.

First published in Great Britain in 2010 by Bloomsbury Publishing Plc.
Published in the United States in 2010 by Bloomsbury U.S.A. Children's Books
175 Fifth Avenue, New York, New York 10010

Library of Congress Cataloging-in-Publication Data
Lum, Kate.
Princesses are not perfect / Kate Lum ; illustrated by Sue Hellard. — 1st U.S. ed.
p.   cm.
Summary: Three princesses, each with a particular skill, decide they are bored with what they do and swap jobs.
ISBN 978-1-59990-432-0 (hardcover) · ISBN 978-1-59990-433-7 (reinforced)
[1. Princesses—Fiction. 2. Self-perception—Fiction.] I. Hellard, Susan, ill. II. Title.
PZ7.L978705Pg 2010   [E]—dc22   2009009324

Typeset in Caslon Antique
Art created with watercolor

First U.S. Edition March 2010
Printed in China by Printplus Limited, Shenzhen, Guangdong
2 4 6 8 10 9 7 5 3 1 (hardcover)
2 4 6 8 10 9 7 5 3 1 (reinforced)

All papers used by Bloomsbury U.S.A. are natural, recyclable products
made from wood grown in well-managed forests. The manufacturing processes
conform to the environmental regulations of the country of origin.

Princesses Are Not Perfect

Kate Lum

illustrated by *Sue Hellard*

BLOOMSBURY

NEW YORK BERLIN LONDON

Once there were three princesses:
Princess Allie, Princess Mellie, and Princess Libby.
They lived in a rose-covered palace by the sea.

They weren't the kind of princesses who sit around
doing nothing. They were very busy. They grew things in
the garden, baked things in the kitchen, and built things
in the workshop. Each princess had her specialty.

Princess Allie loved to bake.
She made the best cakes you've ever
tasted, covered with
royal decorations.
When she baked, she
felt completely happy.

Recipe
Royal
Icing

Pig Palace

Princess Libby loved to build things.
If you wanted anything made, Princess Libby
was the person to ask. When she was
hammering, she didn't think
about anything else.

Princess Mellie loved her garden. She could make just about anything grow, no matter what the weather. When she gardened, she felt all was right with the world.

One sunny morning, the princesses were
sitting in the palace dining room having breakfast.
They were making plans. The next day, all the
children in the princessdom were coming to
the palace for the Summer Party.

Suddenly Princess Mellie, who had not slept very well, said,
"I don't see why I always have to be the one to garden."
The other princesses looked at her in surprise.
"Garden, garden, all day long," complained Mellie. "Dirt here,
weeds there. I am sick and tired of it."

"Well, what would you
like to do instead?" asked Allie.

"Bake!" said Mellie. "I want to bake
things. I'm sure I can bake just as well as you.
Princesses are good at everything."

"But if you bake, what will
I do?" cried Allie.

"You could build things,"
said Mellie. "And Libby could
garden. Don't you ever get
bored, doing the same jobs
again and again?"

"Well, yes . . . once in a while,"
said Allie and Libby.

"Then it's all settled!" cried Mellie.
"I'm the baker, Allie is the builder, and Libby is
the gardener. I'm sure that everything we do will be perfect."

As soon as they had finished eating, they ran to see the housekeeper, Mrs. Blue.

Finest Caviar

Mousse of mouse

Jambon of Snails

Shrimp Bisque

ants à la Crème

Royal Jelly

Coulis for Cats

Truffles of Trotter

POT POODLE

Bluebell

"Mrs. Blue," they announced, "we are switching jobs. From now on, Allie will be the builder. If you want anything made, go to her. Mellie will be the baker. If we need any treats, let her know. And Libby will be the gardener. Go to her for fruits and flowers."

Mrs. Blue looked worried. "Yes, Your Princesses," she said. "But do you think this is a good idea?"

"Of course, Mrs. Blue," said Allie, Mellie, and Libby. *"Princesses are good at everything."*

"Very well," said Mrs. Blue. "Tomorrow is the Summer Party. We will need 100 small baskets of berries."

"No problem, Mrs. Blue," said Libby.

"We will need 100 cupcakes with pink roses," said Mrs. Blue.

"I'll take care of it, Mrs. Blue," said Mellie.

"We will need 100 little chairs," said Mrs. Blue.

"You can count on me, Mrs. Blue," said Allie.

So Princess Mellie went into the kitchen. She looked at the bags of flour and sugar. She looked at the barrels of fruits and nuts.

"Easy as pie!" said Princess Mellie.

And she got to work.

Princess Allie went to the workshop. She looked
at the piles of wood and nails. She looked at the
hammers and wrenches and saws.

"How hard can this be?" asked
Princess Allie. And she got to work.

Princess Libby went out to the garden. She looked
at the hoses and the shovels and the trowels.

"Nothing to it," said Princess Libby.
And she got to work.

Several hours later, Princess Libby
had picked the blueberries.

Princess Allie had built the chairs.

Princess Mellie had baked the cupcakes.

The three princesses limped into the dining room. Mrs. Blue
had prepared a delicious supper, but none of them felt like eating.

"How did the building go?" asked Princess Libby.

"Perfectly," snapped Princess Allie. *"Princesses are*
good at everything."

"How did the gardening go?" asked Princess Mellie.

"Very well," insisted Princess Libby. *"Princesses are good at everything."*

"And what about the baking?" wondered Princess Allie.

"Easy," said Princess Mellie. *"Princesses are good at everything."*

And with that, the three princesses went off to bed.

Princess Allie couldn't sleep. She rolled this way, and she rolled that way. She sighed loudly.

She rubbed her tired feet.

There is only one thing that will cheer me up, thought Princess Allie. *And that is to do some baking!* So she got up, put on her royal robe, and sneaked off to the kitchen.

Meanwhile, in her room, Princess Libby couldn't sleep. She stretched and yawned. She brushed her hair. She brushed her dog.

Finally, she gave up.

"There is only one thing that will cheer me up," said Princess Libby. "And that is a good hour with my tools!"

So she got up, put on her royal robe, and sneaked out to the workshop.

Poor Princess Mellie couldn't sleep either. She tried counting sheep. She tried counting goats. She tried drinking cocoa. Nothing helped.

"The only thing that will make me feel better is to spend some time in my garden," Princess Mellie said with a sigh.

So she got up, put on her royal robe,
and sneaked out to the gardens.

The next morning, all three princesses were late to breakfast. But all three princesses were smiling.

"I had a wonderful night!" declared Libby.

"Best night I've ever had," Mellie said with a smile.

"Yes, it was perfect," Allie said, laughing.

They ate breakfast quickly and ran upstairs to get ready for the children's Summer Party.

By noon, 100 children had arrived. They played games,
ran races, and splashed in the sea. Then Mrs. Blue
called them all into a giant tent.

It was decorated with roses, golden plates,
and piles of treats.

Everything was perfect, except . . .

"Where are the chairs?" cried Mrs. Blue.

"Here they are, Mrs. Blue!" Princess Libby
replied with a laugh.

And she wheeled in 100 perfect little chairs.

Princess Allie stared.

"And where are the blueberries?" asked Mrs. Blue.
"Here we go!" cried Princess Mellie.
And she brought in 100 baskets of lovely blueberries.
Princess Libby stared.

"And what about the cupcakes?" wondered
Mrs. Blue.
"No problem!" called Princess Allie.
And she carried in 100 perfect cupcakes.
Princess Mellie stared.

The children were very happy. They sat in the chairs, they munched the berries, and they loved the cupcakes.

"Princesses make great things," said one little girl. "How can they can do so much?"

"That's easy," said another girl. *"Princesses are good at everything."*

The princesses looked at each other. Then they
started to laugh.

"Princesses," said Princess Allie, "are good
at what they love. You don't have to be good at
everything to be a princess."

"That is very true, Your Princesses,"
said Mrs. Blue. "Very true, indeed!"